For Aimee, Aileen, and Dawn • S.R.
For Katie, Jonny, Sophie, and Amy • S.A.L.

First published in the United States 1998
by Dial Books for Young Readers
A Division of Penguin Books USA Inc.
375 Hudson Street / New York, New York 10014

Published in Great Britain 1997
by Frances Lincoln Limited as *Best of Friends!*
Text copyright © 1997 by Shen Roddie
Pictures copyright © 1997 by Sally Anne Lambert
All rights reserved / Printed in Hong Kong
First Edition
3 5 7 9 10 8 6 4 2

Library of Congress Cataloging in Publication Data
Roddie, Shen.
Too close friends / by Shen Roddie; pictures by
Sally Anne Lambert.
p. cm.
Summary: Hippo and his neighbor Pig are very good friends until
Hippo trims the hedge between their two houses.
ISBN 0-8037-2188-9
[1. Friendship—Fiction. 2. Neighbors—Fiction. 3. Privacy,
Right of—Fiction. 4. Pigs—Fiction. 5. Hippopotamus—Fiction.]
I. Lambert, Sally Anne, ill. II. Title.
PZ7.R5998Too 1998 [E]—dc21 96-48566 CIP AC

Too Close Friends

by **Shen Roddie**

pictures by **Sally Anne Lambert**

Dial Books for Young Readers New York

Hippo and Pig were neighbors. They lived
on a quiet road with a tall green hedge
between their houses.

Hippo and Pig were also very good friends.
On Mondays, Wednesdays, and Fridays
Hippo waddled over to Pig's house for
peppermint tea and chocolate doughnuts.

On Tuesdays, Thursdays, and Saturdays
Pig trotted over to Hippo's for a refreshing mud-bath.

One Sunday, the day they usually stayed at their
own houses, Pig decided to knit a scarf for Hippo.
"It will be finished just in time for his birthday!"
said Pig.

That same Sunday, Hippo decided to do something neighborly for Pig.

I will cut down the hedge between us, he thought. Then we can see into each other's houses and be even better friends.

He got out his shears, set up his ladder, and began to clip the hedge.

"SNIP, SNIP, SNIP!" went
the shears.

"WOBBLE, WOBBLE, WOBBLE!"
went the ladder.

The tall green hedge got shorter and shorter.

"Wallowing walruses!" exclaimed Hippo.
"Now I can see right into Pig's house.
Could that scarf be a present for my birthday?"

Hippo hurried into his house. "I will make
a present for Pig," he said to himself, and he
got out his modeling clay.

Just then Pig looked up from her knitting.

"Fluttering flamingos!" exclaimed Pig.
"The hedge has shrunk!"
Pig stared right into Hippo's house. "What
a pretty mug he's making," Pig said to herself.
"Maybe it's a present for my birthday!"

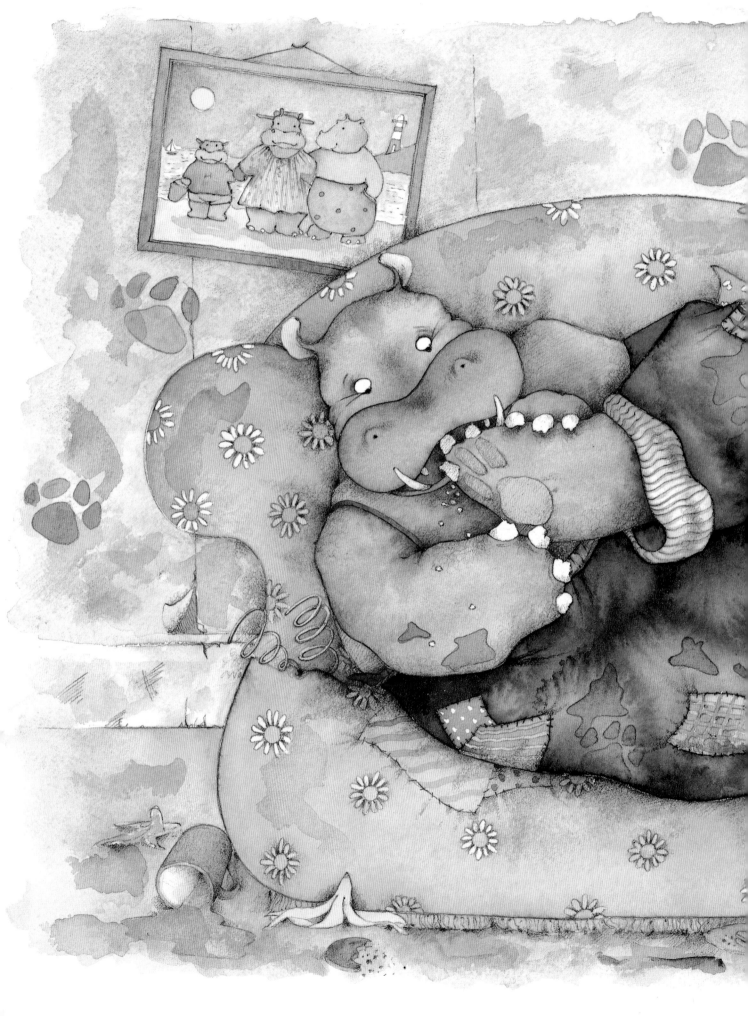

Pig kept watching from her window. She saw
Hippo flop onto the couch and start chewing
his toenails—one by one.
    Disgusting! thought Pig.

Then Pig watched Hippo making lunch
in his kitchen. As he cooked, he kept licking
the ladle and putting it back in the pot.

"Hippo drool!" shrieked Pig in horror, remembering all the bowls of soup she had eaten at Hippo's house. "From now on I'll only eat at home!"

Just then Hippo looked out his window.
He saw Pig rush into her kitchen and pounce
on a pile of doughnuts and cupcakes.

She stuffed them all down in one mouthful!
Sickening! thought Hippo.

"Time for some exercise," said Pig,
belching loudly.

"Dancing is *very* good for the figure,"
said Pig as she sucked in her breath
to button her tutu.

She whirled, and she twirled,
and then . . .

SNAP! The tutu burst and Pig
fell flat on her face.

Hippo roared with laughter. He had
never seen Pig look so funny.

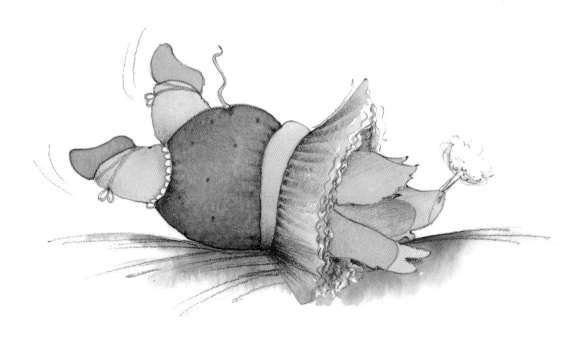

Pig heard the loud laughter. She got up from the floor and looked out her window.

"Hippo!" shouted Pig. "Are you watching me?"

"Yes!" called Hippo. "I saw you stuff yourself with cupcakes and fall on your face."

"I saw you chew your toenails," sputtered Pig, "and drool in your soup!"

"YOU WERE WATCHING ME!" they cried.
"NO, I WASN'T!" they shouted.
"YES, YOU WERE!" they yelled.

Pig yanked her pink curtains across the window.
Hippo shut his green blinds all the way.

Pig and Hippo stopped visiting each other.
Day after day Pig drank peppermint tea
alone in her garden.
Day after day Hippo took mud-baths all by himself.

Meanwhile the hedge
grew taller and taller.

At last it was Hippo's birthday, and Pig was
feeling very sad.

"I miss my friend too much," she said
to herself. "And I am tired of talking to myself!"

So she wrapped up the scarf she had knitted
and carried it next door.

"Hello, Hippo," Pig said shyly. "Happy birthday!"

"What a wonderful surprise!" cried Hippo as he
wound the scarf around his neck. "Thank you, Pig.
You'll never guess what I'm going to give you for
your birthday!"

They both began to laugh.

And because it was a Monday, Pig invited Hippo
over for peppermint tea, chocolate doughnuts,
and birthday cake.

Pig and Hippo were very good friends once again.
But ever after, back in their own homes . . .

they did

exactly as they pleased!